This book belongs to

_____

Backyard Stories

Based on the TV series *Nick Jr. The Backyardigans*™ as seen on Nick Jr.®

SIMON SPOTLIGHT
An imprint of Simon & Schuster Children's Publishing Division
1230 Avenue of the Americas, New York, New York 10020
Surf That Wave!, *Castaways!*, *Riding the Range*, and *Rescue Patrol* © 2006 Viacom International Inc.
Trouble on the Train © 2007 Viacom International Inc. All rights reserved.
NICK JR., *Nick Jr. The Backyardigans*, and all related titles, logos, and characters are trademarks
of Viacom International Inc. NELVANA™ Nelvana Limited. CORUS™ Corus Entertainment Inc.
All rights reserved, including the right of reproduction in whole or in part in any form.
SIMON SPOTLIGHT, READY-TO-READ, and colophon are registered trademarks of Simon & Schuster, Inc.
Manufactured in the United States of America
First Edition
2 4 6 8 10 9 7 5 3 1
ISBN-13: 978-1-4169-3561-2
ISBN-10: 1-4169-3561-4
These titles were previously published individually by Simon Spotlight.
These titles were previously cataloged individually by the Library of Congress.

Backyard Stories

Ready-to-Read

SIMON SPOTLIGHT / NICK JR.
New York   London   Toronto   Sydney

Contents

Surf That Wave!
page 9

Castaways!
page 33

Riding the Range
page 57

Rescue Patrol
page 81

Trouble on the
Train
page 105

Surf That Wave!

adapted by Christine Ricci
based on the teleplay by Janice Burgess and McPaul Smith
illustrated by Susan Hall

Hi! I am Pablo.

I am a surfer.

This is my surfboard.

13

I see a wave.

I paddle my surfboard.

I ride the wave!

Watch this!

I can jump!

I can spin!

25

I can do a flip!

Oops!

Wipeout!

I do it all over again!
I love surfing!

Castaways!

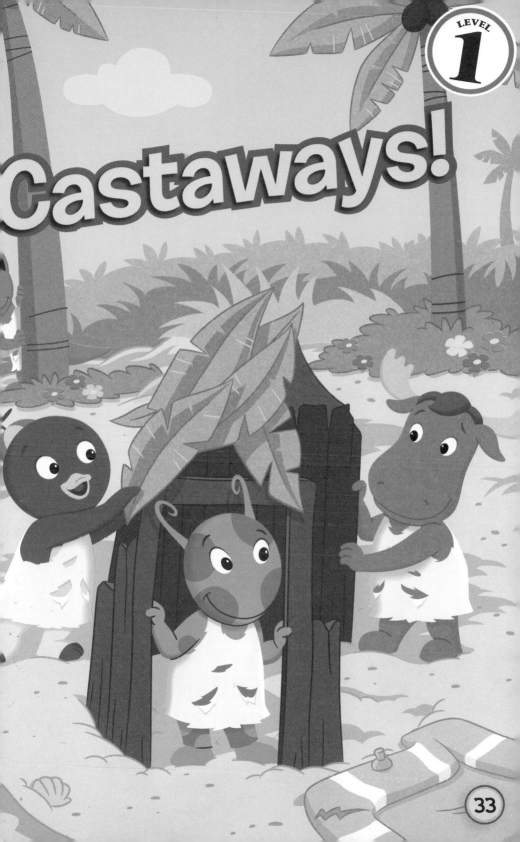

adapted by Alison Inches
based on a script written by Leslie Valdes
illustrated by Warner McGee

"Ahoy, there!" says  UNIQUA .

"Ahoy! We are castaways!"

say  PABLO and  TYRONE .

35

"Our  was lost at
sea!" says .
SHIP
PABLO

"Our  had a leak!"
LIFEBOAT
 adds.
TYRONE

"Now we are stuck on

an 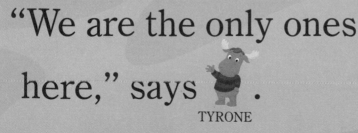," says ....
ISLAND   PABLO

"We are the only ones

here," says ....
                 TYRONE

"I am a castaway too,"

says .

AUSTIN

"I feel very shy today."

38

"I feel too shy to say 'ahoy' to ,

UNIQUA

, and ."

PABLO   TYRONE

"We need to build a  HUT

in case it RAINS !"

says PABLO .

"I will look for WOOD

for the walls."

"Wow," says 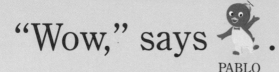.
PABLO

"Where did all of this

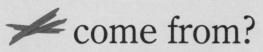 come from?
WOOD

Ahoy! Is somebody there?"

41

"I will look for  VINES

to tie the  WOOD,"

says  TYRONE.

Snip! Snip!

"Hey," calls .

TYRONE

"Who cut these ?

VINES

Ahoy! Is somebody there?"

"I will look for  _{LEAVES} for the roof," says _{UNIQUA}.
Swish! Swoosh!

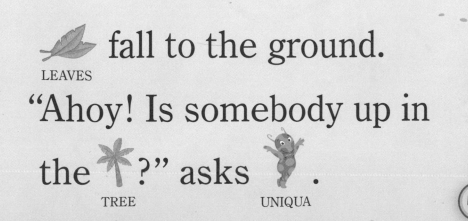

LEAVES fall to the ground. "Ahoy! Is somebody up in the **TREE** ?" asks **UNIQUA** .

The castaways bring the

WOOD   VINES   LEAVES

back to the .

BEACH

They build their 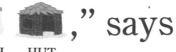.

HUT

"Wow! We built a nice

 ," says .

BEACH HUT UNIQUA

"Now all we need
is food to eat,"
says  .

TYRONE

"Maybe we can
catch a  ," says  .

FISH   UNIQUA

"We can build a ✏️🎣 ,"
FISHING POLE

says 🐧 .
PABLO

"We have a 🪵
STICK

and a 📎 for the hook.
PAPER CLIP

All we need is some 🧶."
STRING

"Hey, where did that  come from?"

STRING

asks TYRONE.

"Ahoy! We are really not alone!" says UNIQUA.

"Follow that 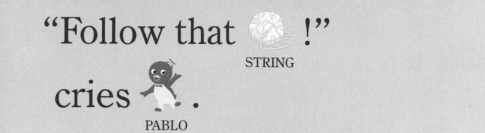 !"
STRING

cries 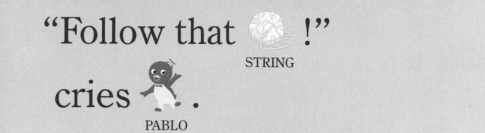 .
PABLO

"Ahoy! Who can it be?"

"It is  !" says .

AUSTIN   UNIQUA

" did all of

AUSTIN

those things!"

" , you should have said

AUSTIN

'Ahoy!'" tells him.

UNIQUA

"I was feeling too shy
to say 'Ahoy!'" says .

AUSTIN

"But I wanted to help."

"That was very nice!"

says .

PABLO

"You are a great castaway."

"Does anyone want a snack?" asks  .

UNIQUA

"Come on! We can have island !"

FRUIT

Ahoy!

Riding the Range

adapted by Justin Spelvin
based on the original teleplay by McPaul Smith
illustrated by The Artifact Group

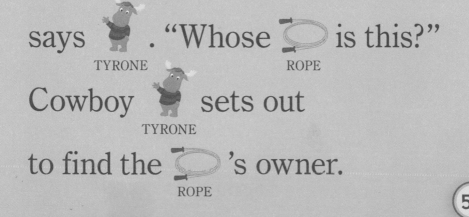

"Yeehaw! I am a cowboy!"

says TYRONE . "Whose ROPE is this?"

Cowboy TYRONE sets out

to find the ROPE 's owner.

"Hey! My  was
ROPE

in the ◣ , but now
SANDBOX

it is gone!" says 🐜 .
UNIQUA

60

"Look!"  says. " !"

PABLO   FOOTPRINTS

"Cowboy made these

BOOTS

!" says .

FOOTPRINTS   TASHA

"There is a bandit

on the loose," says  .

PABLO

"We need to find him!"

 ,  , and

PABLO TASHA UNIQUA

put on their  and climb

HATS

on to their  .

HORSES

63

"The  go into that
TRACKS
canyon," PABLO says.

"It is dark," says TASHA .

, 🦛 , and 🐜 ride

PABLO   TASHA   UNIQUA

into the canyon.

Soon they are lost!

"How do we get out?"

asks  .

TASHA

"The walls are too tall,"

 says.

UNIQUA

66

Then someone calls out,

"Howdy, down there!"

It is Cowboy !

TYRONE

"When your  sees an 🍎,"

HORSE   APPLE

says 🧝, "it will climb out.

TYRONE

🐴 love 🍎🍎!" 🧝 takes

HORSES   APPLES   TYRONE

an 🍎 from his 👜.

APPLE   BAG

68

The  climb toward the 🍎!

HORSES

APPLE

🐧 , 🦛 , and 🐛 thank

PABLO   TASHA   UNIQUA

🦛 for his help.

TYRONE

"We are looking for a bandit,"  says.

PABLO

"But it is too dark to look now," says TYRONE.

"It is time to sleep,"

says.

TASHA

The next day  wakes up

TYRONE

and gets on his .

HORSE

"I will let the others sleep,"

says .

TYRONE

72

As  rides away,

TYRONE

 fall from his !

APPLES   BAG

The other  are hungry,

HORSES

so they follow the !

APPLES

73

PABLO , TASHA , and UNIQUA wake up.

TYRONE and the HORSES are gone!

"The bandit took them!"

says PABLO .

74

 follows the  .

PABLO   TRACKS

 and  follow  .

UNIQUA   TASHA   PABLO

75

"The bandit must be in

that  !" says.

CABIN   PABLO

, TASHA , and

PABLO   TASHA   UNIQUA

tiptoe to the .

DOOR

Then they rush

into the !
CABIN

"Howdy!" says .

TYRONE

 sees 's lasso.

UNIQUA   TYRONE

"That is my !"

JUMP ROPE

"I was looking for the owner,"

says .

TYRONE

 gives the  back.

TYRONE   JUMP ROPE

Then  tummy rumbles.

UNIQUA'S

"We can go to my  HOUSE

for COOKIES ," PABLO says.

"That is good," says TYRONE .

"I am all out of APPLES !"

Rescue Patrol

adapted by Catherine Lukas
based on the original teleplay by McPaul Smith
illustrated by The Artifact Group

"We are Mounties on duty!

We have a big job," says .

TYRONE

"We guard a snow ,"

FORT

says .

PABLO

"Inside the  is a big ,"

FORT   SNOWBALL

says  .

TYRONE

"Yes," says  .

PABLO

"We must guard our SNOWBALL

from SNOWBALL burglars."

85

"We are  patrollers!

<small>SKI</small>

We have a big job!"

says  .

<small>UNIQUA</small>

"Yes," says .
TASHA

"We rescue people

who are stuck

in the ❄❄."
SNOW

"Yum! That hot  COCOA smells good," says UNIQUA .

"We save the ☕ COCOA

for the people

we rescue!" says 🦏. TASHA

" , do you see any

PABLO SNOWBALL

burglars?" asks  .

TYRONE

"Not yet," says .

PABLO

"Do you see anyone who needs help in the ?" SNOW

asks TASHA.

"Not yet," says  .

UNIQUA

"Look! Someone is coming!"

says  .

TYRONE

"Help me close the 🚪 !"

DOOR

94

"I heard a call for help!"

says .

TASHA

"It came from that  !"

FORT

"  patrollers to the rescue!"

SKI

says .

UNIQUA

"To the roof!" says .

"We can see better

from up there!"

"We can climb this ."

LADDER

The  slips on the ice .

LADDER

 and
PABLO   TYRONE

land in the soft .
SNOW

and
TASHA   UNIQUA

pull and
     PABLO   TYRONE

out of the .
SNOW

"We saved you!" says .
TASHA

"Thanks," says  .

PABLO

"We must have scared

away the ⚪ burglars,"

SNOWBALL

says 🐷 .

TYRONE

"We Mounties did our job!"

says .

TYRONE

"We  patrollers did our job!"

SKI

says .

TASHA

103

"Who wants a snack?"

asks  .

UNIQUA

"We have hot !"

COCOA

Trouble on the Train

by Catherine Lukas
illustrated by The Artifact Group

Cowboy  and Cowgirl

AUSTIN   UNIQUA

take a break from herding cows.

"Here comes a ,"

TRAIN

says Cowgirl .

UNIQUA

"That  is carrying
TRAIN

a  of barbecue sauce,"
BOTTLE

says Cowgirl  .
UNIQUA

"The sauce is on its way to Cooking Cowboy  .

TYRONE

He makes the best

BURGERS in the West!"

Someone else

is watching the  too.
TRAIN

"Ready to rob that ,
TRAIN

Bandit ?"
PABLO

asks Bandit .
TASHA

"Yes I am, Bandit ,"
TASHA

says Bandit .
PABLO

111

"I hear there is a
BOTTLE

of special sauce on that !"
TRAIN

says Bandit .
PABLO

"I will use this  ROPE

to try to grab the BOTTLE !"

says Bandit TASHA.

113

"If we get that  of sauce,
BOTTLE

we can become the best

bandit cooks in the West!"

says Bandit .
PABLO

Bandit  twirls her .

TASHA   ROPE

She throws it through the .

WINDOW

She lassoes the  !
BOTTLE

"Look! Bandits!"

says Cowboy .

AUSTIN

"They just stole the  !"

BOTTLE

118

"After them!"

says Cowgirl .

UNIQUA

119

Cowboy  and Cowgirl

AUSTIN

UNIQUA

hop onto their  .

HORSES

They chase the bandits.

"Watch out!"

yells Bandit .

TASHA

" in the road!"

PICKLES

It is too late.

Bandit  and his

PABLO

HORSE

skid and slide on the .

PICKLES

123

Bandit  drops the .

PABLO

BOTTLE

Cowgirl catches it.

UNIQUA

"Good work!"

says a voice.

It is Cooking Cowboy !

TYRONE

"We just wanted to be the best bandit cooks in the West," says Bandit  sadly.

TASHA

"You do not need to be bandits!"

says Cooking Cowboy TYRONE .

"You can be cowboy cooks

with me instead!"

"Yes, sir," says Cowgirl  .

"These surely are the best

in the West!"